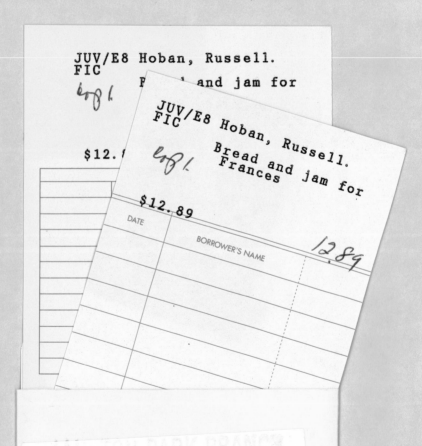

JUV/E8 Hoban, Russell.
FIC
         Bread and jam for
         Frances

$12.89

DATE	BORROWER'S NAME	12.89

BREAD AND JAM
FOR FRANCES

by RUSSELL HOBAN

Pictures by LILLIAN HOBAN

HARPER & ROW, PUBLISHERS

BREAD AND JAM FOR FRANCES

Text copyright © 1964 by Russell C. Hoban
Pictures copyright © 1964 by Lillian Hoban

Library of Congress Catalog Card Number: 64-19605
Trade Standard Book Number 06–022359-6
Harpercrest Standard Book Number 06–022360-X

for Julia,

> who likes to practice
> with a string bean
> when she can

It was breakfast time,
and everyone was at the table.
Father was eating his egg.
Mother was eating her egg.
Gloria was sitting in a high chair and eating her egg too.
Frances was eating bread and jam.
"What a lovely egg!" said Father.
"If there is one thing I am fond of for breakfast,
it is a soft-boiled egg."
"Yes," said Mother, spooning up egg for the baby,
"it is just the thing to start the day off right."
"Ah!" said Gloria, and ate up her egg.
Frances did not eat her egg.
She sang a little song to it.

She sang the song very softly:

I do not like the way you slide,
I do not like your soft inside,
I do not like you lots of ways,
And I could do for many days
Without eggs.

"What did you say, Frances?" asked Father.

"Nothing," said Frances,
spreading jam on another slice of bread.

"Why do you keep eating bread and jam," asked Father,
"when you have a lovely soft-boiled egg?"

"One of the reasons I like bread and jam," said Frances,
"is that it does not slide off your spoon in a funny way."

"Well, of course," said Father,
"not everyone is fond of soft-boiled eggs for breakfast.
But there are other kinds of eggs.
There are sunny-side-up and sunny-side-down eggs."
"Yes," said Frances. "But sunny-side-up eggs
lie on the plate and look up at you in a funny way.
And sunny-side-down eggs just lie on their stomachs and *wait.*"
"What about scrambled eggs?" said Father.
"Scrambled eggs fall off the fork
and roll under the table," said Frances.
"I think it is time for you to go to school now,"
said Mother.

Frances picked up her books, her lunch box,
and her skipping rope.
Then she kissed Mother and Father good-by
and went to the bus stop.

While she waited for the bus she skipped and sang:

Jam on biscuits, jam on toast,
Jam is the thing that I like most.
Jam is sticky, jam is sweet,
Jam is tasty, jam's a treat—
Rasp*berry*, straw*berry*, goose*berry*, I'm *very*
FOND...OF...JAM!

That evening for dinner Mother cooked
breaded veal cutlets, with string beans and baked potatoes.
"Ah!" said Father. "What is there handsomer on a plate
and tastier to eat than breaded veal cutlet!"
"It *is* a nice dish, isn't it?" said Mother.
"Eat up the string bean, Gloria."
"Oh!" said Gloria, and ate it up.
She had already eaten her dinner of strained beef
and sweet potatoes, but she liked to practice
with a string bean when she could.

"Where do breaded veal cutlets come from?" asked Frances.
"And why are French-cut stringless beans called *string* beans?"
"We can talk about that another time," said Father.
"Now it is time to eat our dinner."
Frances looked at her plate and sang:

> *What do cutlets wear before they're breaded?*
> *Flannel nightgowns? Cowboy boots?*
> *Furry jackets? Sailor suits?*

Then she spread jam on a slice of bread and took a bite.
"She won't try *anything* new," said Mother to Father.
"She just eats bread and jam."
"How do you know what you'll like
if you won't even try anything?" asked Father.
"Well," said Frances,
"there are many different things to eat,
and they taste many different ways.
But when I have bread and jam
I always know what I am getting, and I am always pleased."
"You try new things in your school lunches," said Mother.
"Today I gave you a chicken-salad sandwich."

"There, now!" said Father to Frances. "Wasn't it good?"

"Well," said Frances, "I traded it to Albert."

"For what?" said Father.

"Bread and jam," said Frances.

The next morning at breakfast Father sat down and said,
"Now I call that a pretty sight!
Fresh orange juice and poached eggs on toast.
There's a proper breakfast for you!"
"Thank you for saying so," said Mother.
"Poached eggs on toast *do* have a cheery look, I think."
Frances began to sing a poached-egg song:

> *Poached eggs on toast, why do you shiver*
> *With such a funny little quiver?*

Then she looked down and saw
that she did not have a poached egg.

"I have no poached egg," said Frances.
"I have nothing but orange juice."
"I know," said Mother.
"Why is that?" said Frances.
"Everybody else has a poached egg.
Even Gloria has a poached egg,
and she is nothing but a baby."
"But you do not like eggs," said Mother,
"and that is why I did not poach one for you.
Have some bread and jam if you are hungry."
So Frances ate bread and jam and went to school.

When the bell rang for lunch
Frances sat down next to her friend Albert.
"What do you have today?" said Frances.
"I have a cream cheese-cucumber-and-tomato sandwich
on rye bread," said Albert. "And a pickle to go with it.
And a hard-boiled egg and a little cardboard shaker of salt
to go with that. And a thermos bottle of milk.

And a bunch of grapes and a tangerine.
And a cup custard and a spoon to eat it with.
What do you have?"
Frances opened her lunch. "Bread and jam," she said,
"and milk."
"You're lucky," said Albert. "That's just what you like.
You don't have to trade now."

"That's right," said Frances. "And I had bread and jam
for dinner last night and for breakfast this morning."
"You certainly are lucky," said Albert.
"Yes," said Frances. "I am a very lucky girl, I guess.
But I'll trade if you *want* to."
"That's all right," said Albert.
"I *like* cream cheese with cucumbers and tomatoes on rye."
Albert took two napkins from his lunch box.
He tucked one napkin under his chin.
He spread the other one on his desk like a tablecloth.
He arranged his lunch neatly on the napkin.
With his spoon he cracked the shell of the hard-boiled egg.
He peeled away the shell and bit off the end of the egg.
He sprinkled salt on the yolk and set the egg down again.
He unscrewed his thermos-bottle cup and filled it with milk.
Then he was ready to eat his lunch.

He took a bite of sandwich, a bite of pickle,
a bite of hard-boiled egg, and a drink of milk.
Then he sprinkled more salt on the egg and went around again.
Albert made the sandwich, the pickle,
the egg, and the milk come out even.

He ate his bunch of grapes and his tangerine.
Then he cleared away the crumpled-up waxed paper,
the eggshell, and the tangerine peel.
He set the cup custard in the middle of the napkin on his desk.
He took up his spoon and ate up all the custard.
Then Albert folded up his napkins and put them away.
He put away his cardboard saltshaker and his spoon.
He screwed the cup on top of his thermos bottle.
He shut his lunch box,
put it back inside his desk, and sighed.
"I like to have a good lunch," said Albert.
Frances ate her bread and jam and drank her milk.

Then she went out to the playground and skipped rope.
She did not skip as fast as she had skipped in the morning,
and she sang:

> *Jam in the morning, jam at noon,*
> *Bread and jam by the light of the moon.*
> *Jam...is...very...nice.*

When Frances got home from school, Mother said,
"I know you like to have a little snack
when you get home from school,
and I have one all ready for you."
"I *do* like snacks!" said Frances, running to the kitchen.
"Here it is," said Mother. "A glass of milk
and some nice bread and jam for you."

"Aren't you worried that maybe I will get sick
and all my teeth will fall out
from eating so much bread and jam?" asked Frances.
"I don't think that will happen for quite a while,"
said Mother. "So eat it all up and enjoy it."
Frances ate up most of her bread and jam,
but she did not eat all of it.
After her snack she went outside to skip rope.

Frances skipped a little more slowly than she had skipped
at noon, and she sang:

Jam for snacks and jam for meals,
I know how a jam jar feels—
FULL...OF...JAM!

That evening for dinner Mother cooked
spaghetti and meatballs with tomato sauce.
"I am glad to see there will be enough for second helpings,"
said Father.
"Because spaghetti and meatballs is one of my favorite dishes."

"Spaghetti and meatballs is a favorite with everybody,"
said Mother. "Try a little spaghetti, Gloria."
"Um," said Gloria, and tried the spaghetti.
Frances looked down at her plate
and saw that there was no spaghetti and meatballs on it.
There was a slice of bread and a jar of jam.
Frances began to cry.

"My goodness!" said Mother. "Frances is crying!"
"What is the matter?" asked Father.
Frances looked down at her plate and sang a little sad song.
She sang so softly that Mother and Father could scarcely hear her:

What I am
Is tired of jam.

"I want spaghetti and meatballs," said Frances.
"May I have some, please?"
"I had no idea you liked spaghetti and meatballs!"
said Mother.

"How do you know what I'll like if you won't even try me?"
asked Frances, wiping her eyes.
So Mother gave Frances spaghetti and meatballs,
and she ate it all up.

The next day when the bell rang for lunch,
Albert said, "What do you have today?"
"Well," said Frances, laying a paper doily on her desk
and setting a tiny vase of violets in the middle of it,
"let me see." She arranged her lunch on the doily.

"I have a thermos bottle with cream of tomato soup," she said.
"And a lobster-salad sandwich on thin slices of white bread.
I have celery, carrot sticks, and black olives,
and a little cardboard shaker of salt for the celery.
And two plums and a tiny basket of cherries.
And vanilla pudding with chocolate sprinkles
and a spoon to eat it with."
"That's a good lunch," said Albert.
"I think it's nice that there are all different kinds
of lunches and breakfasts and dinners and snacks.
I think eating is nice."
"So do I," said Frances,
and she made the lobster-salad sandwich, the celery,
the carrot sticks, and the olives come out even.

The End